LATE NIGHT SHOTS

A COLLECTION OF STORIES BY

CH

Featuring A Story by Guest Author
Laura Cation

Created with Vellum

For my Great Aunt, who kept me enthralled with the bedtime stories she told me.
Thank you for every single one of them.
I hope mine are half as good.

And for Disney, my special black cat who had a magic all of his own.
This one's for you.

Charlotte

ABOUT LATE NIGHT SHOTS

I have always loved reading short stories.

I HAD the idea for *LATE NIGHT SHOTS* after I wrote my own first short story - a fairy tale with a twist. That story was *SINDERELLA*, and it inspired me to write more 'shorts' alongside writing my first novel.

SINDERELLA NOW APPEARS HERE for the first time in publication alongside two other stories – *GHOSTWRITER* and *THE THIRD DOOR.*

LATE NIGHT SHOTS are intended as short measures of easy reading before the lights go out - each with dashes of mystery and suspense as mixers.

. . .

I HOPE you will enjoy reading them as much as I have enjoyed writing them.

AND I'M pleased to include a story from guest author Laura Cation. *YOU MUST STAY INSIDE* was the winning entry in a 2020 Lockdown Writing Challenge I organised for new writers, never previously published. Congratulations Laura, and I'm thrilled to feature your story in my first collection.

CHARLOTTE V.

GHOSTWRITER

When Fiction and Fact Collide

By Charlotte Valentine

GHOSTWRITER

Alan poured the last dregs of the wine, then gave the bottle a final desperate shake and waited as a few more precious droplets slowly dripped their way into his glass. He couldn't afford to waste any; he needed all the help he could get, especially tonight. And those extra seconds of distraction watching the claret's slow journey along the neck of the bottle were almost as welcome as drinking it would be.

He stubbed his cigarette out and immediately lit another, sat back in his chair and blew exaggerated smoke rings at the ceiling. Hell, he was good at these things; they were still his party piece.

His gaze dropped to the desk. The alcohol and nicotine had worked their combined magic. Now he could focus and finalise his plan. The clock was ticking; he could hear it in his head.

The first decision had been easy - his victim. He'd nailed that in no time. Name, address, occupation, appearance; everything fitted, she was the perfect choice. Now for the rest of it. Time, place, weapon, alibi; every detail must be right.

This had to be the perfect murder.

He woke up hot, dehydrated and disoriented. His neck ached and his lips felt like dried parchment paper. It took him a few seconds to realise he was on his sofa, but he had no recollection of how he'd got here.

He was holding something. His favourite wine glass; lying at an almost ninety-degree angle against the sofa cushion, and virtually empty. He remembered coaxing those last few drops out of the bottle, but he had no idea whether he'd drunk them or just spilled them.

He lifted his head and winced at the pain that shot through it as he looked down at the cream rug that his ex-girlfriend had bought when she moved in - or as he called it, the 'it was cream once' rug. Now it had one more red stain to match the others he'd managed to decorate it with. What the hell had possessed her to choose cream he had no idea; but then Megan had always been the impractical type.

Maybe he should consider dyeing the whole damn rug red. He wished he could take pleasure in the thought of how much that would irritate Megan if she knew, but she never would.

It was too late for her to know. When he called time on the relationship, as he had with all the women in his life, once they inevitably started to want more from him than he was prepared to give, she disappeared. He never made any attempt to contact her of course, that wasn't his style. Once he was done with someone, he was done. But he had been surprised she made no attempt to try again. His other girlfriends always had.

Then six months after their split he learned why. A copy of her obituary and a news clipping had turned up out of the blue in his mail. Megan had died instantly when her car had inexplicably spun out of control late one night on a country road. There was no covering note, so he had no idea who sent it, but it had a London postmark. He assumed it was one of her well-meaning friends. He'd rarely met any of them, and he suspected those he had didn't like him much anyway.

He felt a momentary pang of remorse that he hadn't treated her better, but protracted remorse wasn't his style. And he didn't have either the time or energy for it now.

He sat up, and pain ripped through his head and neck again. This was the worst headache he could remember, and he wondered if this was how being shot in the head felt; he couldn't imagine it being worse.

He squinted his eyes to focus on his watch. He had no idea what time he'd crashed out, but he could see daylight through the gap in the curtains, so it looked like another night of proper sleep missed. His Rolex confirmed it; 9.30 am, even worse than he thought. His eyes lingered on the diamond embellished dial; one of the trappings of success.

The watch had been his gift to himself when his second book had topped every bestseller chart that mattered, and he began making serious money from his writing. How good that had felt, and how much worse it made everything feel now.

Now that he struggled to write even a decent sentence.

He forced himself to swing his legs off the sofa and stand up. He needed coffee, lots of it, and at least two paracetamols. He prayed he hadn't run out as he lurched his way dizzily towards the kitchen. He glanced at the desk as he walked past it. The blank screen of his laptop seemed to give him an accusing look, even in its sleep mode. He wondered if he'd actually written anything last night before crashing out.

Time to find out after some caffeine and painkillers, although he suspected he knew the answer.

He looked across the room at his bookshelves, and there he was, in pride of place, with a shelf to himself. Evidence of the good old days. Hardback and paperback versions of his three bestsellers; his name emblazoned on the spines. Alan Dale, three-time winner of Crime Writer of the Year. He walked back to the desk and pointed his finger at the blank screen of his laptop.

'You smug bastard. See over there? All written before you came along. So much for you being an upgrade.'

He walked into his kitchen trying to blank out the memory of his fourth book. He didn't want that one on his shelves. Unfortunately, hardly anybody else did either. Critics had savaged it; and his normally loyal readers, who'd bought the two follow-ups to his debut novel in droves, had hated it.

He threw water and a capsule into his expresso machine, and as it gurgled into life, promising imminent caffeine, he heard his phone vibrate against the worktop. He could guess who this would be. Only his agent called or messaged him before ten these days. Everybody else knew better.

He tapped the screen and pulled down the notifications alert, so Roger wouldn't know he'd read the message. He needed thinking time before the call he knew would come later.

Roger had left an early voicemail and now a text message. He was clearly anything but a happy agent.

Alan still felt raw from their last conversation, two days ago. Roger had hurled Alan's thirty pages on the desk in his smart agency office and leaned back in his chair.

'So that's it? Six months, and that's what you bring me?

You think I can bullshit my way through a meeting with the publisher with that pile of garbage?'

Alan had squirmed with discomfort in his seat, like a schoolboy being chastised in front of his classmates. Somehow his agent's Australian accent could imbue the word 'garbage' with a level of invective the Queen's English could never come close to. He stammered out a reply.

'Look Rog, I know it doesn't look like much, but...'

'Doesn't look like much? Alan, let me spell this out for you one more time. They're pretty much done with you and your delaying, full of excuses, crap. A six-book deal, one a year, remember? You don't need me to remind you what a disaster book four was. And now book five is already overdue.'

'I know but...'

Roger held his hands up. 'No more 'buts'. I've done all the trading on your former glory I can do. That last best-seller was two years ago - ancient history now. If we can't get at least ten chapters of this new one, and a more inspiring plot outline than you've produced so far, to them in a week from now – max - they'll pull the plug.'

He paused and looked Alan in the eye. 'Is this getting through to your hungover brain? Stop looking for inspiration in the bottom of a bottle and just write the goddamn thing.' He leaned forward over the desk and pointed at Alan. 'Because either you email me those chapters four days from now, and on day five you're sitting in front of me with hard copy, or you're sitting in front of me with a termination agreement on the desk. Clear?'

Alan looked down at his hands. They were clammy and he thought he might be sick. Four days. Back in the day he could've produced twenty chapters in that time at a push. But at the rate he was writing at the moment...

Yet this was at least a reprieve of sorts. He looked up at Roger and nodded, trying to fake a level of confidence he didn't feel. 'Crystal clear. I'll see you in five days. I'm on it.'

Now here he was in his kitchen, half his reprieve time already gone, and he had no idea what kind of progress report he could give Roger. He couldn't even remember if he'd written anything last night before he'd collapsed on his sofa. Time to wake up the smug bastard laptop and find out.

He carried his coffee to the desk, opened the laptop and keyed in his password. The document containing his novel sprang into life, but he didn't recognise the words that appeared on screen. He looked down at the word count. Bloody hell. It had tripled from when he'd last seen it.

His heart raced as he started to scroll back through the document. He couldn't believe what he was seeing. Somehow, he'd got the manuscript of his book nailed to the end of chapter ten, and a quick read told him it was good, maybe some of the best writing he'd ever produced. Especially the murder scene. The last thing he remembered was agonising over that, and now here it was; dramatic, meticulous in its details. It was perfect. He absorbed every word as if he was one of his readers, not the guy who'd written what he instinctively knew was a brilliantly conceived crime any writer would kill to have produced. Including him up until last night.

He smiled at his own pun. He really had pulled off the perfect killing in Chapter 9, and God knows how he'd found the inspiration for it, but there it was. At last he had a novel on his hands. He just needed to stay in this groove now and another bestseller beckoned. Perhaps his most successful yet.

His mobile rang. Roger, bang on cue. For the first time in

weeks Alan hit the green button to answer straightaway. Let his agent tell him this was garbage when he emailed it to him.

'Roger, I hope you're sitting down. I've got good news, and...'

'Good news?' Roger didn't even let him finish his sentence. 'You Brits and your love of the understatement. Alan, this isn't good, it's fantastic! I've read it twice since it landed in my inbox right after my earlier voice message. This is dynamite, mate; one of the best things I ever read. Best murder scene for sure; I felt every moment of it. You took me right inside the killer's head. We've got ourselves a winner here.'

Alan caught his breath half way through Roger's words. When the hell had he emailed his agent these? He opened his email account and scrolled to his Sent folder. There it was; timed at 8.30 am. When as far as he knew he'd been comatose on his sofa, spilling wine and dead to the world. In no condition to have done anything.

Roger was speaking again. 'Look, get yourself showered and come in to town for lunch. I'm going to whack this straight to the publisher. Forget hard copy, I don't need to change a damn thing. So, I'm buying...mate, you there?'

Alan mumbled a response. 'Erm...give me a rain check on lunch. Pulled a pretty late one last night. I need some sleep.'

He hit call end without waiting for a response and slumped down in the chair, still staring at his laptop screen. He realised he was shivering, although his body felt warm. His earlier elation had been replaced by a discomfort he didn't recognise.

Maybe he really did just need sleep. But he couldn't drag his eyes away from the email to Roger. How could he not remember something he'd typed and sent less than two hours ago?

Something wasn't right, and he had no idea what it was.

He woke up and looked at his watch. 3pm. Hell, he'd been out cold for hours, but at least he felt better. God knows what all that weirdness had been about earlier. Writing the perfect murder had obviously screwed with his head.

In the kitchen he downed half a carton of orange juice. That and a hot shower should make him feel human again. Then he'd capitalise on last night's success and press on with his manuscript. He couldn't afford to lose momentum now he was back in the writing zone; there was too much at stake. He'd played Russian Roulette with his career, but he'd survived, and he wasn't going there again.

A familiar bleep startled him, and he swung round to face the desk. The laptop should be in sleep mode, but it wasn't. It had woken itself up, and it bleeped again as the blank screen sprang into life. What the hell was going on with it now? He walked towards it ready to type in his password, but he didn't need to. He blinked in disbelief as his manuscript flashed up. He looked at the word count, and he froze.

It had doubled.

He started reading the new words. They were as brilliant as the first ten chapters, and he had no recollection of writing them. He looked away for a moment and glanced round the room. He had no idea who or what he was looking for, but some inexplicable pang of guilt had hit him - as if he was spying on someone else's book. A book that had been written by somebody he didn't know.

Somebody who was a way better writer than he would ever be.

Alan couldn't remember the exact moment he decided not to care how new words were being added to his novel daily, at a rate he'd never achieved before. He only cared that it was happening.

He convinced himself he was having these flashes of brilliance in some semi-conscious state during the long hours he seemed to crash out after a bottle of wine. Every time he slept, he woke up to find himself one step closer to a finished book. A better book than any of his others.

And it had all led to this moment. Sitting in London's premier bookstore, one of the most prestigious in the world; with his book taking pride of place in the window. '*OUT OF NOWHERE*' - which he knew was a more apt title than anybody else could imagine - had stormed its way to the top of every bestseller list within its first week. Even before its release the odd teaser from it, and a brilliant ad campaign conceived by Roger, had sent pre-orders through the roof. Now the publisher couldn't print copies fast enough.

This was his first public signing event for this book, and fans were queuing around the block for a copy of it, and the opportunity to meet him. He'd always hated these events with his previous books, and - worse - tonight marked the beginning of a particularly hectic nationwide tour of them.

He looked up from the pile of books in front of him and tried to force a smile he didn't feel.

'What name shall I dedicate it to?'

He found himself staring at yet another expectant female face giving him the coy come-on look. It irked him, as that look always did, but then he was no stranger to female attention. It had been a constant from the moment he hit his late teens and suddenly morphed from boy to man overnight. From then on, he'd always had his pick of women.

Not that he was particularly nice to them. Constant availability had turned him into an arrogant bastard; he had to admit that even to himself. One of his more outspoken conquests had told him 'he wore his arrogance like a badge.' She hadn't lasted long, but he knew she was right.

And he wrote that same arrogance into his fictional villains; there were more than a few bits of him in all of them. Aside from the killer aspect; that flawed part of their personality he invented. Over the years, as he wrote his killing words, he sometimes wondered how killing another human being might actually feel...

The woman in front of him giggled her reply. 'Could you make it "With love to Linda", please? I want to make my friend jealous. She couldn't get here today.'

He gave her the most enthusiastic 'Of course Linda' he could summon up and tried to ignore the signals she was obviously trying to send him.

As if she was remotely his type. He preferred them blonde and willowy, and the woman in front of him was anything but either. He hadn't seen anybody in tonight's crowd of clamouring fans who was his type - and he wouldn't touch this one if she'd arrived gift-wrapped with a bow.

He was finding this signing session hard work. It had gone on for two hours already. His right hand ached, as did his face from the constant forced smiling and he could use a drink. As he looked up to speak to Linda, he saw the queue still extending way beyond the bookshop's entrance. God he could be here for hours yet. As soon as he dispatched Linda he'd insist on a break.

'I think I'm probably your biggest fan. I've been to the signings for all your books. I love them.'

He rewarded her breathless enthusiasm with the grateful author smile that he'd practiced over the years and hoped he was giving a convincing impression that he remembered her. He signed his name with the flourish he'd also perfected and held the book out to her. She took it from him with one large, gloved hand and held the other one out to him. He gave it a brief absent-minded handshake and mumbled an indifferent 'thank you' and 'enjoy the book' as he scanned the room looking for Roger and a temporary escape.

Before he could spot his agent, his attention was drawn to a smartly-dressed figure at the back of the waiting queue. He froze as the woman the figure belonged to stared at him, her eyes blazing into his.

His hand gripped the desk. This wasn't possible. It was Megan, his ex-girlfriend who he'd treated so badly just months before she'd been killed.

And she was looking very much alive.

A hand touched his shoulder. 'Bloody hell, mate. You alright? You look like you've seen a ghost'.

He turned to reply to Roger, but no words came. He looked back at the waiting line of fans, wanting to check what he'd seen, but he was too late. Megan had gone.

Roger was talking again. 'Let's take a breather Alan; looks like you need it. Grab yourself a coffee and get some air. Give your signing hand a rest. I'll make an announcement and get some more wine rustled up for these guys still waiting. OK?'

Alan relaxed his grip on the table as he nodded. 'Some

air would be good.' He added a mumbled 'Mind's starting to play tricks on me, I think.'

His agent grinned. 'Yeah. You suddenly looked a bit rough. Take fifteen minutes and get yourself back on track.'

Alan grinned back. 'Occupational hazard of being a writer, I guess. Overactive imagination sometimes. Seeing things that aren't there. But I'm good. Just need that breather.'

He turned to grab his jacket from the back of the chair, picked up his phone and reached for his personalised signing pen. It wasn't there. Alan checked the floor, his jacket pocket in case he'd slipped it in there, but no – it was gone. Then he remembered Linda, whose book he'd just signed, and her excited expression when he handed it to her; he guessed she'd helped herself to his pen as an extra memento. She wouldn't be the first fan to do that; it had happened on his previous book tours and he generally shrugged it off, but tonight it annoyed him. He looked around the shop and tried to spot her, but without success.

She'd gone too.

~

He woke up, realised he couldn't feel his legs, and tried to think why. Images of Roger flashed into his head. The two of them, late night, tequila shots, lots of. Boy, had they got through a few. He vaguely remembered trying to call a halt at some point, but Roger had insisted and had kept on buying.

'Come on, mate. Not every day you break the signing record for the world's most famous bookstore and top a couple of new release bestseller charts. Think we've earned a few of these.'

The combination of alcohol and salt had made him wake up desperate for water, but he had to convince his legs to move first. He had zero recollection of either getting home or into his bed, and he wondered if he'd managed it single-handedly or whether Roger had been forced to help him with both. He wasn't sure he wanted to find out.

He stood up on shaky legs, staggered into his living room and got his answer. His agent was comatose on the sofa, one arm dangling as if it almost didn't belong to his body. Alan tried to laugh but it made his face hurt. It seemed unlikely Roger had taken charge last night, so God knows how either of them had made it back to the flat. An obliging Uber driver he assumed.

He walked to the kitchen, filled the kettle to make tea and hit the TV remote. He had some fanciful notion that his record-breaking signing session might have made the news. He half listened to a report on the latest middle-east skirmish as he hurled tea bags into two mugs while the kettle boiled, then span around as he heard the word London.

But as the opening words of the breaking news from the capital sank in, he yelled over the reporter's voice. 'Roger, wake up. Now. We've got a problem.'

He watched the screen, transfixed by the images being shown. As the reporter continued speaking Alan shivered as his blood ran cold. The kettle shook in his pouring hand and he screamed as boiling water hit the fingers of the other one which seemed stuck to the mug handle with the force of superglue.

'Jesus, Alan, what the hell?'

He was barely aware of Roger rushing into the kitchen and snatching the kettle from him as he continued to pour boiling water on his own fingers and hand. He was almost numb to the pain of the cold water that Roger plunged his blistering fingers into. He was oblivious to everything but the horror of the words in the news report.

Roger hit the pause button on the remote as he forced Alan to keep his hand in the water.

'Calm down mate. Bloody hell are we hungover. Couple of accidents waiting to happen today I reckon. How's the hand feeling? Give it a couple of minutes in the water and...'

'Screw the hand Roger.' Alan reached for the remote, hit live rewind, then play. 'Listen to the goddamn report. Then tell me to calm down.'

Ten minutes later they sat in stunned silence at opposing ends of Alan's sofa. Roger spoke first.

'It's classic copycat. It's unbelievable.'

Alan's eyes were still locked on the tv screen as he forced his equally locked mouth to move in a reply.

'Unbelievable? Try surreal. Every detail. Every bloody one. Right there on the screen.'

He'd replayed the live news story several times over, watching in morbid fascination; part of him not quite able to comprehend the images he was seeing and the words he was hearing.

A young woman's body discovered in West London. The victim of a particularly vicious murder. The detective at the scene, a senior officer whose lined face bore the hallmarks of a man hardened over the years to the very worst of human behaviour, appearing visibly shaken as he described what he'd just seen as 'Evil. Pure evil.' Almost identical words to those Alan's fictional detective had used about a fictional killing.

And now fiction and fact had collided head on. The victim's name. Her appearance. The location where she'd been found. The brutal manner of her death. Brutality described so expertly in the chilling words of Alan's book.

Words that people had been reading for days. Words that everybody thought were his; and that only he knew might not be.

More than might; he was convinced they definitely weren't. How that was even possible, he had no idea, and his blood ran cold again. Because if he hadn't written the words then one other person knew it - the writer who had.

And that thought now left him feeling twice as uncomfortable.

Alan wasn't surprised when the video entry system buzzer in his hallway sounded an hour later.

He shot a glance at Roger, but for a minute neither of them moved. They hadn't spoken for the past thirty minutes. Alan had spent most of that time being ill, and the rest of it wondering how he was going to deal with the complications he'd created for himself when he'd passed off somebody else's words as his own - complications he couldn't believe he hadn't predicted. How stupid had he been?

On top of that he was still reeling from the statement Roger had made earlier as he snatched the TV remote from Alan and hit the off switch.

'No point watching this over and over mate. It's time to focus and decide how we capitalise on it.'

'Capitalise on it? What the hell are you talking about? This is a disaster.'

'Disaster? Are you kidding me?' Roger had waved his mobile at him, as it pinged twice. 'Twenty emails on here already and I'm guessing those pings make it twenty-two.

That's how much of a disaster this is. TV and movie offers coming at us like machine gun fire. This is big, Alan.'

Alan stared at him. 'Big? And people call me an uncaring hard ass. A woman just died for Christ's sake - and all you can think of are movie deals?'

Roger laughed in his direction. 'Give me a break Alan. Don't get all moral and ethical for the first time in your life, and don't try to pretend the same thought didn't cross your mind. Whatever I think, and whatever we do from here on, doesn't change what's happened or bring a murdered woman back to life. And I didn't invite a bunch of offers; these guys came to me. What do you suggest I do? Ignore them?'

Alan held his hand up. 'I don't want to talk about it.'

'Well you can forget that as an option. The press will be rocking up here any minute and you're going to have to talk about it. We need to control the message, so we'd better figure out what it is; and quick.'

Bile rose from the depths of Alan's stomach as he imagined a barrage of cameras and microphones being thrust at him. He made it to the bathroom just in time as spasms of nausea wracked his body until he collapsed on the floor, clutching his head as pain shot through it. The taste of last night's tequila sent nauseous waves crashing through his system again. He gripped the edge of the sink and prised himself up on legs that refused to stop shaking. He used one hand to cup water from the tap. He alternately drank it and splashed his face with it until he cooled down, then squeezed toothpaste onto his finger and rubbed his teeth and mouth until mintiness masked the still lingering bitter sensation of alcohol.

He saw his reflection in the mirror and gasped at the contrast between the face staring back now and the one that had headed out of the apartment last night - the successful heartthrob author about to be greeted by his adoring fans replaced by a haggard, middle-aged man who suddenly looked older than his years.

Now he suspected he was about to be front and centre of a different media frenzy. He closed his eyes and took some deep breaths; he'd better be ready for it.

He headed back to Roger. He was going to need his agent's help to hold this together.

Although he was expecting it, Alan jumped as the loud buzz signalling a visitor broke into the silence.

Roger was the first to speak. 'It begins. I'll get it, and I suggest you get some coffee on the go. You look like shit, and I'm guessing I do too.' He stood up and tapped Alan on the shoulder as he walked towards the video entry system control panel. 'I know this is a shock but remember we're on the same side here. I was a bit bloody insensitive earlier maybe; it's the blunt Aussie in me. But I'm here to support you.'

Alan gave him a weak smile. His agent could be blunt, but he was damned effective at his job, and after all these years they knew each other inside out. Their relationship had gone way beyond agent and client; they were close friends, and he'd never been more grateful to have a friend by his side than he was now.

He stepped onto his balcony for air before he walked to the kitchen. There they were, thirty floors below him; the gathering hordes of reporters. Before they caught sight of him, he moved back inside, but not before he saw the police squad car. He guessed he should have anticipated they wouldn't take long to get here.

For once he was pleased at the slowness of the building's lifts; at least he had a few minutes to get some caffeine on the go and compose himself before they made it up to the thirtieth floor.

Alan found himself staring into the lined face of DCI Philip Reynolds. He felt he knew every one of those lines, given the number of times he'd replayed the man's news interview at the murder scene.

Reynolds was clearly an old-school detective. He didn't stand on ceremony or waste what he obviously thought was valuable investigating time exchanging polite pleasantries. He cut straight to the chase.

'Well Mr Dale, we have ourselves quite an interesting situation here, don't we?'

Alan tried to look unfazed as he nodded his reply. 'I realise that. A copycat killing.' He paused as he gulped down the discomfort and embarrassment that rose up in him. 'I could never have imagined my words would lead to this. This type of thing just... just doesn't happen. To think that of all the people who've now read my book, one of them has...' He stopped; he didn't want to hear himself admit that the torture his fictional villain had inflicted on his victim had been re-enacted in real life.

He felt guilt radiating from his every pore. Guilt for being a fraud, and guilt that his fraudulently acquired words had led to a real-life death.

Reynolds continued in his matter of fact tone. 'Yes. Let's talk about readers for a minute. How many people have read your book so far?'

Alan raised an enquiring eyebrow at Roger, hoping that

when his agent answered the question, he'd keep any hint of triumph out of his voice.

He needn't have worried; Roger kept his tone factual and neutral. 'Well it's been out less than two weeks and it's sold just over a hundred thousand copies. About a third of those in the UK; the rest overseas. Alan has a pretty big international following.' He paused. 'Guess that's a lot of suspects.'

Alan shot him a look, then turned back to Reynolds, assuming he'd be unimpressed with the last line, but the detective muttered a barely audible 'Not necessarily' before firing another question. 'Let's go back to timing for a moment. So, you published this book just under two weeks ago.' He didn't even pause to acknowledge them nodding in response. 'Now tell me how many people had seen it before that? From what little I know about your business a book goes through a lot of people before it sees the light of day. How many with this one?'

Alan frowned and shifted uncomfortably in his seat. Where was the guy going with this?

Roger answered instantly. 'Actually, with '*OUT OF NOWHERE*' very few saw it before publication. Because we knew it would be hard hitting and it has - let's say - an unusual ending, we decided to keep it pretty much under wraps. We didn't want any spoilers out there. We sent out some very brief extracts to our usual reviewers, but we just gave them a teaser basically. Not the usual complete book to read in advance. Beyond that just a very limited group - me, a handful of senior guys in the publishing company, plus a couple of editors, proof readers, typesetters. Not much more than about twenty in total I suspect.'

The detective turned to Alan. 'Interesting you chose not

to reveal the identity of the killer at the end. That's pretty unusual, isn't it?'

Alan nodded. 'Very unusual, which was kind of the point of the novel. To show that life, death and crime can be totally random. Even the best investigation doesn't always lead to a neat symmetrical outcome.'

The DCI gave him a stony stare. 'Maybe not in your world Mr Dale, but in mine it generally does. I usually get my man. And I will this time.'

Alan decided to soften his tone. He had the distinct impression Detective Reynolds had taken an instant dislike to him and it probably wasn't too smart to make a bad situation worse. 'Well anything I can do to help, obviously. I feel a sense of responsibility here because of the similarity to my book and...'

He was interrupted as a mobile phone rang. One of the junior officers took the call and muttered a 'Yes, I see.' into it before leaning down to whisper something in his boss's ear. Reynolds nodded and turned to Alan.

'Well Mr Dale, it seems things have got a little more complicated than that. Can you tell me where you were on the twenty-second of May between ten and midnight?'

Alan caught his breath. Where was this going? He had no idea where he'd been on a Tuesday night over two weeks ago, but unless he'd been in a late pre-publication meeting, he suspected he'd probably been crashed out on his sofa, oblivious to the world. And he feared that wasn't going to make for an ideal answer. He stammered a reply. 'I...I've no idea, I'd have to check. Possibly alone here. Why? And what does "a little more complicated" mean?'

'It means I've just learned we have some evidence that appears to link you to the crime scene.'

Alan choked on his next words. He told himself he must

have misheard. 'What? Did you just say, "linking me?" What could there possibly be that links me?'

Reynolds stood up and looked at Alan as if he expected him to stand up too. Then he spoke in a tone that chilled Alan to his core. 'I think this would all be better discussed at the station. I suggest you take a few minutes to decide if there's anybody you need to call. There's no telling how long this could take.' He turned to Roger. 'If you can shed any light on Mr Dale' movements on May twenty-second, I suggest you let us know as soon as possible.'

Roger stepped forward, put his hand on Alan's shoulder and gave Reynolds a challenging glare. 'Now hang on just a moment. This is crazy. Alan can't possibly be involved or implicated in any of this. All he did was write a book for Christ's sake. Something that I just told you a shitload of people have been reading for...'

Reynolds held his hand up, gesturing for Roger to stop, and Alan winced at the look the detective gave him.

'Well here's the thing. Actually - they didn't. In your words, no more than about twenty people did. You see, by the time your client's book was published to the world two weeks ago, our victim had already been dead for a week.'

~

From the moment he walked into the police station, Alan somehow knew how this scene ended; the way he would write it if he was a character in one of his novels. Which in a way he felt he was; in a strange convoluted quirk of fate, his fiction had become his fact.

Finger printing, DNA swabs; the intermittent flickering of the lights on the interview room's tape recorder. Alan knew every step of how this worked; he'd done his writer's research on police procedures. The hardened detective interrogating him, with the rookie detective alongside trying to impress his boss. Like stereotypes from his books - characters now brought to life in front of him. The irony of the situation didn't escape him.

And the plot unfolded exactly as he feared it might. Forty-eight hours after he walked in, he was formally charged with the murder of Naomi Louise Wilson.

The name had meant nothing to him, but in the last two days his interrogators had repeated it to him incessantly, as they'd shown him picture after picture of her mutilated body - a body mutilated in the same savage and barbaric fashion that he'd described so realistically in his book. Mutilations made all the more gruesome by the fact that Naomi had lain undiscovered for almost three weeks.

Time passed in a blur of little sleep, intermittent nicotine when Reynolds gave him a smoking break, and no alcohol. The more he was questioned and confronted with evidence that made no sense to him, the more confused he became, until even he began to doubt his own innocence.

All those hours he'd spent blacked out in his flat; so much time when he couldn't account for his movements, either to the police, or to himself. Those hours when his book had been mysteriously written. What else might have happened during those hours that he wasn't aware of? Could he be capable of something unimaginable? He didn't know anymore.

When he was given time alone in his cell, every thought was invaded by the words of his book. Words he now feared were destined to haunt him for the rest of his life. Words he should probably confess to never writing. But he couldn't bring himself to do it.

Until the evidence against him became increasingly

damning, as Reynolds cleverly and systematically introduced strands of evidence that shook Alan to his core. Inexplicably they all placed him in Naomi's home.

Their first discovery had been a personalised pen, customised with his book title and his name. Roger had commissioned several for Alan's exclusive use on the book tour, which he'd presented to Alan when they'd finalised the tour details a month ago. Nobody had touched them but him, except on one occasion...

He calmly explained that one identical to it had gone missing at his book signing. But Reynolds was unimpressed and raised a sceptical eyebrow.

'Suggesting what Mr Dale?'

'Suggesting that somebody planted it at the scene. To implicate me.' He knew his explanation sounded limp and stupid as he voiced it.

The rookie sidekick smirked at Alan's obvious discomfort and Reynolds simply laughed.

'Are you suggesting a killer went back three weeks after committing a murder for the sole purpose of planting your pen at the scene? Hardly sounds likely does it?'

'Well somebody out there must have done. Because if you're suggesting I put it there, I...'

The still smirking junior detective leaned forward in his seat and interrupted him. 'There were no prints on it apart from your own and the victim's. Been showing off to Naomi a bit, had you? Trying to impress her as the big-shot author about to go on tour signing his bestseller. I mean she was your type, wasn't she? Suppose you thought that'd get you a bit of action.'

Alan wanted to scream. How dare this jumped-up jerk accuse and belittle him, trying to impress his boss. Temper and fear rose up from the pit of his stomach with a combined force that threatened to choke him. He wanted to rewrite this scene now. It needed to end with him walking out of this place. 'I keep telling you! I didn't know Naomi Wilson, so I wasn't trying to either impress her or seduce her! Why won't you guys believe that? And what's all this "my type" crap?'

Reynolds responded to the outburst in his matter of fact tone. 'Let's not worry about what we believe at the moment. We're here to go through our evidence and get some answers. No more, no less. It's what we owe the poor woman whose mutilated body is now lying cold on a slab. And I will find out who did this. And why.' He paused and turned to the rookie who passed him a plastic evidence bag which he held up to Alan. 'Do you recognise the box inside the bag?'

Alan gulped. 'Yes. It's the box the personalised pens came in.'

'Pretty exclusive make; can't have been cheap. How many were in the set?'

'Four. I only used one.'

Reynolds shot him a questioning look. 'Really? You see, that's interesting. Because when we recovered this box from your desk there were only two in it. What do you suppose happened to the other one?'

Alan's temper erupted and he slammed his fist on the table. 'I've absolutely no fucking idea! None! There were four pens. I used one. Maybe I lost one; maybe somebody took it. Whatever happened to it I didn't leave it at an apartment I've never even been inside! What sort of a stupid bastard would do that? And by the way, I've changed my mind. I want to call my lawyer; I want him here, now!'

Reynolds nodded and leaned over to switch off the tape machine with a resigned 'Interview terminated at 17.05.'

'I think that's a good idea Mr Dale. We'll take a break and resume when he arrives.'

Alan stared nervously at the man sitting opposite him in the private interview room they'd been given. He and Nick had met at university, become firm friends, and stayed in contact ever since. Nick was now a partner in a top city law firm and Alan trusted him completely.

'So, what are they likely to throw at us next Alan? I know how this guy Reynolds works. He's good. And he doesn't go on hunting expeditions, so trust me; he has a lot more in his kit bag than missing pens, or you wouldn't be here. I suggest you tell me what it might be.'

Alan clenched his hands together until his knuckles turned white. If Nick, as both lawyer and friend was nervous about what other evidence the police thought they had, he should be too.

'Nick, I have no idea. This whole thing's a nightmare. I never met this woman. I've been nowhere near her flat. And I had nothing...absolutely nothing... to do with her death. All I did was write a book. That's it; there is nothing else. Anything the police think they have can only be circumstantial, or somebody's trying to implicate me. You have to trust me. And...' He stopped himself in mid-sentence.

'And?'

Alan looked down at his hands; he had a choice now. Should he confess to Nick the mystery of how the book got written? Within seconds he told himself not to; he wasn't ready to do that yet. He knew how disastrous the fallout would be.

'No, it's ok. It's nothing. Tell them we're ready to resume.'

They sat side-by-side in the interview room. Reynolds and a young female detective, who at least seemed less smarmy than her predecessor, sat opposite. Their faces were expressionless as they stared at Alan who was still in shock from their latest revelation.

Fingerprint and DNA evidence placed him all over Naomi Wilson's flat - and all over her. An empty bottle of wine full of his fingerprints, despite a seemingly clumsy attempt to remove them. Two glasses in the sink, equally clumsily rinsed.

Everything bore the hallmark of a killer out of control; both the frenzied nature of the attack, and the random, unsuccessful attempt to get rid of the evidence.

Alan had no answers; he was baffled. He wanted to wake up from this nightmare. Roger had been unable to provide any information about where his client might have been on the night the murder was deemed to have taken place.

More lost hours in the life of Alan Dale.

Several people had been questioned by the police and attested to the fact that this was a frequent occurrence after he drank. Alan's heart sank at the ironic realisation that he had thousands of fans as a writer; but pitifully few friends as a man. In truth, apart from Roger and Nick he seemed to have no allies.

This couldn't be any worse.

And then came the hammer blow.

Alan was still reeling from the letters he'd been shown; letters that his ex-girlfriend Megan had apparently written in the weeks leading up to her death but had never sent. Letters that described the way Alan had treated her; his frequent violence towards her; his threatening behaviour when he drank; and his inability to remember where he'd been, or what he'd done, when he sobered up.

He read them in disbelief. None of this was true. But there was no doubt the handwriting was hers. He knew it, and it came as no surprise that several people had already confirmed that it was. He turned to Nick and asked for a break to speak privately. The time had come, and now he had no choice; he had to tell his lawyer the truth.

A truth that would damage his career irrevocably, but a truth that might save his life.

Of course, it didn't do any good. If anything, it made matters worse.

How had he ever expected anybody to buy a story about words "magically" appearing on his computer? And, of course, nobody did, including his lawyer. Not only did they not believe him, but it sounded like either the last desperate attempt of a sane, but guilty, man to protest his innocence; or an insane man reinforcing his evil madness.

The police indulged him by agreeing to Nick's request that the laptop be examined, but no evidence emerged of it having been tampered with or hacked. Alan was at the end of the road.

He stared down at his hands as this particular scene ended with the words he'd feared for two days.

'Alan John Dale. I'm formally charging you with the murder of Naomi Louise Wilson…'

~

'Would the accused please stand.'

Alan stood up on shaky legs he wasn't sure would support him. The fear pulsing through his body weakened him, weakness compounded by several weeks of incarceration while he was on remand awaiting trial - eating prison food and refusing to use the prison gym. He'd lost weight and strength; his once-toned muscles were wasting away.

He leaned forward and gripped the polished mahogany of the dock as he bowed his head; he was broken. He knew how this final scene ended too. He'd known how every scene ended since the morning he saw the news report of a murder that had become front-page news and had led - as some part of him had always known was an inevitability - to this moment.

When he heard the request to the jury foreperson to stand, he knew the verdict was a foregone conclusion. Alan barely heard the word 'Guilty', or his barrister's request that the judge await further psychiatric evaluations before passing sentence. He was only aware of two pairs of strong arms that gripped both of his to lead him back to incarceration.

And that's when he saw her.

Looking exactly as she had the last time he saw her. His Megan look-alike. Elegantly and discreetly dressed, a large hat pulled low over her face. As he looked at her, she raised her head just enough for him to be certain it was her. She nodded her head and a flicker of a smile illuminated her face briefly before she turned to leave the courtroom - disappearing within seconds of him noticing her, as she had in the bookstore. But that smile had imprinted itself on him.

It was a smile of triumph.

Alan barely left the security of his cell. Killers of women and children were unpopular and at risk of rough justice from their fellow inmates, so he only ventured out when a guard escorted him to his fortnightly session with one of the team of psychiatrists. They played around with different medications, which he knew he didn't need, but was forced to take. He'd stopped even listening to their explanations of his treatment.

They were convinced he was delusional, and he no longer cared what they thought. They were tranquilising him too; their attempt to calm his anxiety attacks and reduce his agitation level - agitation he knew would never leave him. He was constantly consumed by his own desperation to know who had done this to him.

He was convinced somebody had. Someone who was clever; extremely clever. Clever enough to have pulled off the perfect crime, and to have fooled everybody.

Apart from Roger he received no visitors, nor did he want any; he'd lost all interest in the outside world. He'd stopped reading the press; he couldn't deal with the phenomenon his book had become. Sales of *'OUT OF NOWHERE'* had skyrocketed into the publishing stratosphere. They had from the moment he'd been charged with murder, and the guilty verdict had driven them even higher.

The public couldn't get enough of how fact and fiction had become one and the same thing; the book's success seemed limitless and unstoppable. A movie deal had already been concluded. Money beyond his wildest dreams was piling up in the business account Roger and his team now managed for him. Money that he would probably never spend.

He sat for hours staring into space; on his knee one of the many notebooks Roger had brought in for him.

'Try to get through this by writing mate. It's what you do. It'll help.'

He'd given his agent the best smile he could. The notebooks and pens were a well-intended gesture, but Alan knew he would never fill them. So far, in three months he hadn't written a single word, and he doubted he ever would again. Although he felt compelled to check every morning to see if any words had appeared during the night.

They never did.

The woman stepped back after she carefully arranged the flowers she'd brought. Pink stargazer lilies; they'd always been Megan's favourite.

She smiled at the sight of them as she pulled her wide-brimmed hat lower to protect herself from the summer sun; they were the perfect flowers for Megan. Her sister had always been a bit of a stargazer herself. That's how she'd got herself mixed up with that bastard in the first place. Full of some naïve notion that she could tame the arrogant womaniser who didn't give a damn about anybody, or anything, but himself and his success.

Her expression switched from its softness when she thought about her sister, to a hard look of pure hatred when she thought about him - Alan Dale, the successful writer. Success he'd somehow managed to achieve with those God-awful books of his. Formulaic garbage in her opinion, but garbage that had appealed to the masses, with no literary merit whatsoever.

Until his last book. She smiled an ironic smile; now that one really did have everything. Thanks to her, of course. And it all been so easy.

She looked at Megan's headstone and remembered when she had decided to do it; the precise moment the plan had started forming. It had been within seconds of the police telling her about her sister's accident. An inexplicable crash on a quiet country road; a car assumed to have spun out of control. But she knew better; it had been no accident. She knew what Megan's state of mind was in the weeks leading up to it; this had been deliberate.

She didn't tell the police any of that. They probably wouldn't have believed her if she had. They would have filed it as sisterly grief talking and brushed her theories aside. And then he'd get away with it. She wasn't letting that happen; she had a far better idea. And she knew how she'd make him pay. She would hoist him up with his own arrogance and thirst for success, and she'd hang him with them.

She had done exactly that, and all it took was for her to harness her extraordinary combination of brains, technical skills and self-discipline. Hacking into his computer so expertly that the police morons would never be able to detect she'd done it. Writing a murder that she planned every detail of; and then committing it for real. Picking a victim who exactly matched her requirements; a loner with no job, no family and few friends. Someone who could lie dead undiscovered for three weeks until the police received an anonymous call from a concerned 'friend' which would lead them to a gruesome early morning discovery.

And above all, a victim who looked his 'type'. A woman he'd be hard pressed to deny he'd pursued. That had been tough; it had meant her stalking, and ultimately killing, a Megan look-alike. But she'd done it; she'd had no choice.

Just as she'd had no choice but to train herself until she could copy Megan's handwriting perfectly. The letters she'd then painstakingly produced had been the prosecution's final trump card. How she'd enjoyed those being read out by the QC and seeing the mystified look on Alan Dale's face. A look only she'd known was genuine. The jury hadn't bought it for a moment.

And, of course, she'd had Megan's spare keys to the bastard's apartment. They made it so easy to rummage around and gather all the things she needed, when he was completely oblivious after yet another drunken binge.

The empty wine bottle, the glasses, the fancy pens. What a nice unexpected bonus those pens had been. She'd disposed of one of course; how she'd enjoyed that part of the plan. Disposing of something that would be wrongly assumed to be a key bit of evidence linking him to the scene. Because she needed to plant one of its identical partners from the set - the one he started to write with first, with his prints all over it. The one she wouldn't be able to get till the very last minute, almost three weeks after she killed Naomi.

It was the only thing that could have gone wrong with her entire plan - the timing of it, and the risk she'd taken to get it; hiring the over-sized Linda, who'd never even heard of Alan Dale. But Linda was happy to be paid well for ten minutes' work pretending to be a fan, some quick sleight of hand to steal the pen, and an enthusiastic handshake to get Dale's DNA all over one of the brand-new gloves she'd been given to wear.

She hadn't planned to kill Linda; just to pay her off. But after she planted the pen at Naomi's flat and rubbed the glove over Naomi's stiff, mutilated corpse, she changed her mind. She felt the occasional pang of guilt about getting rid of the poor woman, but after killing once, killing again had been surprisingly easy to do. And she couldn't afford Linda to be a loose end.

She read the words on Megan's headstone, as she'd done so many times. 'Beloved sister of Angela.' They'd been all the words it needed; there was nobody else to mention. And nobody else who could have righted the wrong of her sister's death.

She bowed her head and whispered. 'I did it, Megan. I made him pay. We won.'

Angela turned away to walk back to her car. She didn't know what her future held. She wasn't sure if she'd ever go and visit Alan Dale and tell him what she'd done. A part of her wanted to see him; to experience her moment of triumph in front of him. But when she'd looked at him in the courtroom and given him that smile, she sensed he knew.

He could never know for certain of course, unless she decided to tell him. And that pleased her. The thought of him having to live with the constant frustration of knowing somebody had done this to him. Someone cleverer than him. But never truly knowing exactly who, or why.

She liked the idea of that gnawing away at him. Then one day, when he'd suffered enough, she might even write this as a story. Under an assumed name, and as a work of fiction.

A work of fiction that he'd know was true.

But for now, she'd leave him to live with his frustrations until the day came that she needed him to know; needed him to know that she'd beaten him.

But that could wait. For now, it was enough that Megan knew that she had.

Angela glanced back at the stargazer lilies tilting their heads towards the sun, and her sister, and she smiled.

SINDERELLA

If The Shoe Fits...

By Charlotte Valentine

SINDERELLA

How ironic it was that the shoes had led him to her - at the end and in the beginning.

Her smile twisted at that thought as the police car drove her away. She glanced round and saw him, his face impassive as he stared back at her. Her Prince Charming, who had become her captor. The one person she hadn't been able to fool.

As the car sped through the town centre and the Church clock struck midnight, she noticed some late Trick or Treaters returning home, scurrying through the cold Halloween night like scampering mice. The distorted jagged grins on their still flickering pumpkin lanterns mirrored that twisted smile of hers as she thought back to where it all began, to once upon a time...

Sindy sat at her usual corner table in The Palace Club, the Friday night go-to haunt for anybody who was anybody in her town. She was in her standard pulling outfit - the tight bodycon dress, just the appropriate amount of bling, and, of course, the heels.

What was it about heels that worked every time? Her practiced eye worked the room for some fresh male prey as she tried to ignore the inane prattle of the two other women at the table. Her ugly, stupid stepsisters. Every moment she spent with them was an endurance. Hatred rose up inside her like bile and she took another sip of her dirty martini to wash the taste of her anger down.

'Take your sisters out on the town, Sindy. And be nice.' her father had said. Be nice? She detested both of them. They'd invaded her world, them and their even more stupid mother. The perfect world she'd created for her and her father. She was his golden girl, his princess. What Sindy wanted Sindy got. It had always been that way. Until the invaders showed up.

Now she was expected to share him, and Sindy didn't do sharing. Nor did she intend to for much longer.

Seeing her father's lawyer leave the house two days ago had been her tipping point. The visit could only have meant one thing. He was obviously changing his will, and Sindy wasn't letting that happen. She needed to do something, she needed to do it fast, and she needed it to be foolproof.

She couldn't pull something like this off on her own of course, but she knew exactly who to go to for help. Her phone pinged with the message she'd been waiting for and she turned away from her giggling companions to open it.

It was the answer she wanted. Her meeting with the Fairy Godmother was confirmed for tomorrow. She looked back at the sisters and inwardly shuddered at their dowdy uncool outfits. But she gave them her best fake smile. This nightmare would soon be over, and she could play nice for one more night.

She downed the rest of her martini and glanced towards the bar. And there he was, leaning against it. Tall and dark, manly physique, just her type. He looked bored by his companions too and as he turned away from them in her direction, she made eye contact with him. His eyes lingered, as male eyes always lingered when they stared at her.

There was an instant connection as he surveyed her and the sisters. He seemed to recognise a fellow boredom sufferer and a smile flickered across his face. Sindy gave him the coy look she knew never failed and casually tossed her blonde hair - another of her weapons of mass destruction. She watched his eyes work their way down the tight dress and the long legs to the heels, and knew she'd nailed her prey for the night.

Later, with the sisters safely dispatched in an Uber, she learned he was Steve, a newly appointed DCI and newly divorced. She also learned he liked blondes in high heels. The irony of his occupation didn't escape her as she thought about what she was planning. Hell, he'd probably wind up being the investigator - what a deliciously fun prospect that was.

She'd better get this relationship as physical as possible, as quickly as possible, and hook him before Police protocol got in the way. As they left The Palace and his arm slid round her, she suspected that was going to be deliciously fun too.

~

When she walked into the Fairy Godmother's apartment the following morning, she was still feeling the after-glow from her night with her DCI. Their encounter had been urgent, raw and mutually explosive. The cocaine hit she was now anticipating would truly be the icing powder on the cake.

As usual the transaction was swift. Money for powder, nice and simple. And the FG only ever supplied the best. But today they had other business to discuss too.

'It's all set Sindy. It happens tonight. It'll be done by midnight. Then you go home and find them before your father gets back. You do all the things we agreed, and you don't try to get clever.'

Sindy listened as the blow began to work its magic and the familiar euphoria pervaded her senses. She always loved the feeling of invincibility it gave her. It was one more reason why she needed the invaders gone. This was an expensive indulgence, and one she couldn't live without.

~

She chose that night's stilettos especially carefully. She had a plan in mind for them apart from turning her detective on again. He'd been messaging her all day, and she'd enjoyed winding him up with increasingly raunchy replies. He'd be the perfect prelude to tonight's main event.

Once she was ready, she timed her coke hit perfectly so she sparkled just enough without being obvious. She rechecked with the invaders that they were staying home. She didn't want any last-minute glitches now. Thank God they were reality tv freaks. Their night was mapped out, or so they thought. As she walked to her cab, she smiled a coke-enhanced smile at the prospect of what lay ahead for them.

She wowed Steve again of course. He really was pretty hot, and such a leg and heels man. He couldn't get enough of her. Pity he was going to be busy over the next few weeks and didn't even know it yet. But having him around was going to add a nice touch to proceedings she thought. Who knew that murder plotting could be such fun?

The text came just before midnight. It was done. Perfect timing. She disentangled herself from her more than satisfied sleeping detective, got dressed quickly, and texted his number to let him know she was leaving. His phone pinged as her message arrived, but as she'd expected he didn't even stir. He'd be getting woken up sooner than he thought and would see it.

Then she slipped on her shoes and quietly let herself out.

~

As she approached home, and the security lights signalled her arrival, she thanked God for chemically-induced calm. She unemotionally let herself in and headed for what she knew awaited her. She heard the tv and saw the flickering images of the screen through the open sitting room door. She walked in on a home shopping presenter espousing the virtues of the latest magic mop. God the shit these women had watched.

She imagined she smelled the blood before she saw it, sweet and cloying even to her drug-impaired nostrils. And then her eyes took in the death tableau, the three of them tied together, motionless and flopped against each other on the sofa, like discarded shop window mannequins.

The Fairy Godmother's man had followed the brief exactly. Three perfect executions, and three problems solved. Sindy's three wishes granted.

Time for her to do as she'd been told now, flip her phone on and make the emergency call. But she couldn't. Not yet.

She'd fantasised about how this might feel for too long. She needed to enjoy the moment first.

She removed one shoe and gripped it tightly. Her face contorted into its twisted smile as she looked at the three lifeless bodies in front of her. Then she raised her arm and rained repeated blows on their heads until her madness was satisfied.

And now, as the police car continued its journey, she thought how perfect life could have been after that night, and how it almost was.

How solicitous Steve had been throughout the investigation. An investigation that concluded this was a particularly vicious drug-crazed crime by perpetrators unknown. How she'd comforted her father through his grief and become his princess again.

But how then, against all the odds, the shoes were found. She remembered the look on Steve's face when he'd taken a late-night call about their random discovery

and the gruesome appearance of one of them.

And the final indignity tonight, when he'd forced her to try her foot in that right shoe. Looking into his eyes as she knew he was thinking of the last time she'd worn them for him. The time that could have been the start of their Happy Ever After.

But that only happened in fairy tales.

She sank back into the warmth of the police car and smiled her twisted smile again.

YOU MUST STAY INSIDE

Going outside was Joel's only hope...

By Laura Cation

COPYRIGHT

DEDICATION

To mum and dad who always taught me to do my best at everything.
I miss and love you both so much.

YOU MUST STAY INSIDE

His head hurt. He thought he could hear a pounding siren somewhere. Was that really surprising for London?

Joel Connor opened his eyes slowly to find himself on the floor of what looked like a stock room, staring at the spine of "1984" by George Orwell. On the other side he was met with Aldous Huxley's "Brave New World". As a fanatic of classic books, he had read both eagerly by the time he was eight. Now, at ten years old, it was somehow reassuring to be reunited with them, especially in the confusion he found himself in.

Wait a minute. Now he remembered. His mum sounding panicked. Angry voices telling her she shouldn't be out. Her pushing him into this room out of sight. The virus. They were taking a chance being out, being seen - but she just wanted to spoil him, give him some escapism from this awful pandemic taking over the capital.

A mysterious virus had come from nowhere. Appeared in the form of orange smoke. An unusual smell. A virus that hit your immune system, infected your blood stream. If you refused isolating yourself away from society, away from others...death was the only option - or being put into compulsory isolation by the pandemic police.

They were everywhere in the city.

Getting up, he looked around. Absorbing his favourite smell. Old antiquarian books...seeing his favourite sight; shelves of books in dark, cosy alcoves in the "Absolutely Antiquarian and Coveted Collectible Bookshop".

Sitting curled up in a corner of his bedroom with a classic novel was all he wanted to do: a loner not interested in "Fortnite" or the latest craze on "Tik Tok". He thought about his mum. Where was she now? Try. Try to remember. Sadly, his mind was writing a blank page.

Joel looked out of the window feeling a wave of uneasiness. No one. Nothing, except...silence. He couldn't even work out whether the alarm he had heard before had stopped, or perhaps his mind was playing tricks. He felt the familiar sensation that had come over him so often before. Chest tightening. Dry mouth. Short...gasps...for...air.

'Keep calm, count to ten...it's fine, you just need to see what's happening. You're fine.' he kept saying to himself in his head.

He stepped outside the shop and looked along Marylebone High Street. No one in sight. His heart started pounding again as he put one foot in front of the other, heading away from the familiar - the comforting presence of books, to, what had appeared to be an eerie emptiness. An area of London suddenly devoid of cars, buses...PEOPLE.

'Hello?' he called out. 'Hello?!'

A little louder now. Almost echoing. Again, all he was met with was silence. Walking along further, a flier blew down at his feet. Picking it up, he read three words emblazoned on it: "You are warned." He read on to the small print:

"You are unsafe in London. There is a virus that will attack your immune system and result in rapid death. You must stay at home. Anyone found disobeying this instruction will face the wrath of the pandemic police."

Joel had heard his classmates talking about the virus at school but hadn't really paid any attention.

The teacher would sneeze. 'Hey watch Miss! You've got the virus! Don't give us it!' they sniggered.

Now he felt a rising panic at the dilemma of heading back to the shop to stay safe or keep going to find his mum. He decided. Keep going. He had to find her. Had to know for sure. A voice came from nowhere making him jump:

"Deaths caused by the virus now at 1,272...vaccine to be produced in July. Please remember if you are found outside you will be punished severely. We see everything."

As quick as it started, the message came to an end. Sounding like it had come through an old, crackly speaker.

Joel found himself outside "Madam Tussauds" waxwork museum. The sign on the door said "Museum temporarily closed. Virus is spreading. Please stay at home."

It was bizarre to see no queue outside halfway round the block. Turning away he came face to face with two figures. He gasped seeing them dressed in white with hoods and visors attached and wearing white surgical gloves. Face to face with pandemic police on patrol.

'You are not supposed to be out!' one of them announced, slightly muffled. 'You will need to be punished!'

His mind went back to how it all began. This voice sounded like the one he heard in the book shop shouting at his mum.

Joel tried to make a run for it, but he had no hope with these two, barely identifiable figures grabbing an arm each. They put a blindfold over him and pulled him along.

'Help!' he cried. 'Someone?!'

They scoffed beside him. 'Do you seriously think anyone will hear you?! That there will be anyone out?! You should know this is why YOU must be punished!'

'But I...'

'Silence! We will hear no more of this!'

Joel felt the wave of panic again rise up from his stomach. As they pulled him blindly along, he had no idea where they were taking him. He was now indeed facing the wrath of the Pandemic Police. He felt himself flying and landing on what appeared to be a pile of rubbish bags.

'You will stay here now until we decide what we will do with you!'

~

The door slammed shut and he whipped off his blindfold. Before he could think about his anxiety, he heard a voice emerge from a corner.

'Who's that? Is there someone there?'

The comforting voice he knew so well evaporated all the panic and confusion.

'Mum? Mum, is that you?!'

'Joel?? Oh Joel, I'm over here! Can you crawl over to me?'

Eagerly he crawled over to where he heard her voice, finding her looking pale but overjoyed to see him.

'Oh Joel! I am so pleased to see you! I hope you understand why I had to leave you there?'

'Yes. I do...but now they have found us both and I have no idea what will happen!'

They could hear a rustling sound across from where they were sitting, and a light appeared from nowhere shining on to a mouse that was crawling around. Then Joel saw a gap, big enough to crawl through. His mum turned to him.

'Joel! Do you see that gap? I'm sure it will be big enough for us to get through, what do you think?'

'Yes, I see it...and anything is worth a shot right now!'

He followed his mum over to the gap, crawling behind, looking at his hands from time to time, checking there were no more mice around. He wasn't keen on mice, but all that should matter now was getting out of here. Carefully they inched through the gap, feeling puddles underneath their fingers and a stench of raw sewage.

'Are you OK Joel?' she asked him every five minutes or so.

'Yeah, mum, I'm fine...just keep going!'

It felt like forever. Somewhere, in the distance, even more muffled now was the crackled speaker.

"Deaths caused by the virus now at 2,500...vaccine to be produced in September. Please remember if you are found outside you will be punished severely. We see everything."

It was almost on a loop, but with different information now on when a vaccine would become available...death rate rapidly increasing.

They continued their slow crawl; this was like a tunnel, with twists and turns. He felt they would never reach the end of this long passage...but then a glimpse of light.

'Look Joel! We're nearly there!' his mum gasped.

'Yes!' he replied, but already wondering what was on the other side.

They moved forward faster now, shuffling along on their elbows.

'Here, Joel...we can get out now!'

His mum dropped down on her hands and edged her way towards the light until her legs finally went through last. Joel followed her with her easing him out. Looking around they saw they were on Baker Street. She took his hand.

'Come on! We have to make our way home from here without being seen!'

They hurried along a desolate Baker Street. A car with four blown tyres. A child's pram left. An abandoned briefcase. Glancing at him slowing down to look, Joel's mum stopped.

'Joel, we don't have time to look around now...we need to keep going, come on! You've been doing so well!'

Moving quickly again, they heard something behind them. Footsteps. Joel gasped.

'Mum! I can hear someone behind us!'

'Keep going, come on...we need to speed up! Let's run!'

He kept up with her. The Pandemic Police, no doubt. His chest tightened.

His mum gasped suddenly.

'Joel? Can you smell that?'

An unusual smell in the air, something he could not even describe. Nothing he had smelt before.

'Yes! Mum, can you see that in front of us?'

Orange smoke. Twisting and turning as if caused by smoke from a fire.

'Joel...I can't breathe...'

'Mum...I can't either, what's happening?'

They both sank to the ground. Gasping for air. Feeling their eyes smart. As they lay on the pavement two white figures appeared beside them.

'We told you to stay indoors…' they said, just as a crackly message came over the city again.

"Deaths caused by the virus now at 2,502...vaccine to be produced in December. Please remember if you are found outside you will be punished severely. We see everything"

THE THIRD DOOR

What lies inside...

By Charlotte Valentine

THE THIRD DOOR

Evie hit the snooze button on her phone again and pulled the duvet over her head. She always needed at least three snoozes to psyche herself up to face a Monday morning, but at least this one was Christmas Eve. She only had to get through today then she wouldn't have to face another Monday until next year. She certainly had no intention of setting her alarm and working on New Year's Eve. Not that she'd got a plan for that night yet, but she was working on it.

Which explained why she felt particularly worse for wear this morning, even by normal Monday standards. She knew it served her right for Tindering too late last night, but it had been worth it. She'd spent hours swiping left, then suddenly - voilà! - she'd right swiped on a really hot guy and to her delight 'It's a Match' had flashed up on her screen.

Even though she was still half asleep she smiled as she remembered his profile photo. After her next snooze she'd take another look, and if he still looked hot in the cold light of day, she'd send him a 'Hi' message. Maybe things were looking up.

Which was more than she could say of her latest job -

Junior Trainee to the Senior Trainee at "Bartholomew & Bartholomew", Estate Agents. They were now the only agents in Colville, which she privately and guiltily called "Dullsville", the small market town she'd grown up in and couldn't seem to escape from. Although she conceded that its lack of excitement to her spelled charming to others.

It was a pretty place, which attracted plenty of weekend visitors, but it amazed her when out of town house hunters stared at the property photographs in the shop window, then walked in and asked her for more details. She took more interest in the people who just casually looked at the photographs, carried on walking and never came back. She wished she could do that.

And she wished that, just once, something exciting would happen in Dullsville.

~

An hour later Evie drove her dilapidated Renault through the equally dilapidated gates of Beechcroft Manor, an old Victorian pile on the outskirts of town.

She was here to do her first solo write-up on a new listing. It was an 'opportunity' the older and slightly lesser dull of the Bartholomews had told her. She'd stifled a grin and tried to make her 'Thank you' sound sincere.

She stared up at the house through her windscreen, reluctant to leave the warmth of the car. Whoever had named this place had clearly suffered from delusions of grandeur. She'd arrived expecting imposing and intricate, but what she got was the plainer end of classic Victorian. Red brick, double-fronted, with twin gables like isosceles triangles. Boring in its symmetry. Hardly Victorian splendour.

The dark clouds looming overhead didn't help the house's kerb appeal, and she frowned, wondering where they had come from. It had been sunny only minutes before when she turned off the main road and into the private drive - more by luck than judgement, as her sat nav had unusually played up and refused to locate this place.

Glancing at her watch as she got out of the car, she shivered at the sudden drop in temperature as icy air assaulted her. She gripped the driver's door for support and gulped as her nostrils froze and her lungs hurt when she took a breath. She contemplated getting back in her car, driving away and calling the office with some excuse. But she didn't want the label of Junior Trainee forever, so she leaned back into the car and took one deep breath in its still relative warmth, held it, and grabbed her bag. Then she hit central locking and ran towards the house.

Bartholomew Senior had given her two hours for this job, but he could forget that. She had other ideas. She'd go in and note down what she could, room by room, as quickly as possible. And she'd take plenty of photos on her phone she could refer to later. Thirty minutes tops. Then back to town, a coffee stop, and a chance to hit on Mr. Tinder. After a night's sleep, she'd decided he looked even better, and he was definitely a New Year's Eve candidate. And getting this job done quickly would leave time for some last-minute Christmas shopping. Maybe she'd check out that red dress she'd spotted at the weekend. That would be perfect to wear for Mr. Tinder. She grinned in spite of the cold. She had a whole week to work on him.

She swore at the front door as her numb, blue fingers struggled to keep their grip on the keys, which refused to turn in the lock. When had anybody last used them? Ages ago, judging by the pile of free newspapers and circulars she found herself pushing against when eventually she got the keys to work. Paper information seemed to breed in Colville – the online world hadn't quite reached it yet. Most of its residents had clearly missed that memo.

She stepped across the paperwork into a dark hallway and closed the door quickly. She expected some light from the landing window but there was none. She felt for the light switch with her icicle fingers but hitting it had no effect, so she switched on her phone torch.

She looked around as if she was an opportunist burglar casing the place, but a quick glance told her it was no burglar's dream. Shabby, and obviously uncared for, this cupboard was definitely bare. She and the Bartholomews would struggle to give it the welcoming walk-in feel all house hunters wanted, but at least it had the archetypal Victorian colourful tiled floor and central staircase. They could play those up, and maybe she could find a few more redeeming features as she walked around.

She decided to head to the room on the left first. The house layout looked straightforward, with two doors either side of the hallway and one at the rear, which she assumed was the kitchen. More boring symmetry.

Twenty minutes later she'd punched details of each progressively more unremarkable room into her phone. Beechcroft Manor was a series of uninspiring square boxes. It had no vibe at all, manorial or otherwise. It was lifeless. And totally silent. It didn't even have the musty smell she'd expected to find in an empty house. In fact, she wasn't conscious of breathing in air at all.

And then it hit her. This place was completely sensation free. Since she'd walked in, she'd observed, noted and photographed. But she hadn't heard, smelled or really touched anything. She was in a vacuum, a sensory void.

Apart from one feeling that was seeping through her entire body.

Unease.

She shivered against it. She wanted to get out of this house. She glanced at her watch and saw it had stopped. Her damned phone battery was running low too. She was sure it was at full charge when she walked in. Now this place was really freaking her out and she couldn't wait to get out of it.

She headed towards the door and stopped as she caught sight of herself in the hall mirror. At least the image that stared back looked like her. But the reflection was so much older. It was as if her mother was gazing into her eyes. What the hell was going on? She turned away and hurried to the front door, but before she opened it, she took one last look behind her.

And that's when she saw it. A light from under a door to the right. How could that be? None of the lights had worked. Telling herself not to, but unable to stop, she walked back towards the light.

And realised the symmetry was suddenly all wrong.

This was a third door. She hadn't seen this door before, and now it disturbed the pattern. But it was drawing her in.

She reached out, and slowly turned the handle.

~

As the door clicked open, Evie hesitated. Her eyes, accustomed to the house's darkness, blinked as the light from this room burned into them. She turned away from it and looked back at the hallway. She told herself to run to the front door, get out of this place and drive into town as quickly as she could. The familiarity of Colville's predictable dullness was suddenly appealing, in contrast to this house which was playing games with her that she didn't understand.

She tried to move her hand, but she couldn't. The door handle seemed to be gripping it, like iron filings being pulled to a magnet. Without her pushing it, the door creaked further ajar. The same magnetic force compelled her to move towards the light, and she was powerless to resist it.

'Come in Evie. I've been waiting for you.'

Evie's stomach lurched with the sickness of fear as a woman's voice came out of nowhere.

As if it knew her thoughts, the voice spoke again. 'Walk through the door Evie and don't be afraid. On the other side is your destiny. Here. Inside the room. Trust me, and don't fight this.'

Without her telling them to, her feet crossed the threshold. As she stepped into the room, the door closed behind her. She turned to see a key turning in the lock and heard its click. She reached out to touch it, but it deflected her hand like a force field.

'You can't escape Evie. The room won't let you.'

She looked in the direction of the voice. It came from the back of the room, but her view was blocked by a semi-circle of mirrors which faced her. She could see nothing else.

A floral sweetness hung heavily in the air and it seemed to pervade her pores. She recognised the smell. Jasmine. It felt familiar, but she had no idea why.

When eventually she could speak through the cloying sickliness of the scent, her voice shook. 'What is this place? Who are you? Why am I here?'

'So many questions Evie. Walk into the circle and you'll get your answers.'

'Who are you?'

'You already know who I am Evie. You just don't realise it yet. But you must look into the mirrors. These mirrors are your life. Your past, and your future.'

Evie's heart skipped a beat, and for a moment she thought it had stopped. Again, she wanted to turn and run, but her feet refused to move, and she stammered her reply. 'What...what if I don't want to see my future?'

'You have no choice but to see it. Just like I had no choice. Now enter the circle. The room won't let you go until you do.'

Evie turned her head back towards the door, and gasped as she was faced with a blank wall. Any means of escape was gone. She had no choice but to follow the voice. She walked into the circle, the room light dimmed, and she turned to the first mirror on her left as an image slowly appeared in it.

It was her. A happy little girl running, laughing and giggling in the garden. And there was her rabbit. She watched herself pick him up and hug him to her. She'd called him Bunny and he'd been her best friend. Tears pricked her eyes at the memory of how much she'd loved him, and she reached out to the mirror, wishing she could touch him, but the image began to fade.

She turned to her right as she saw another image appear. She smiled at the mirror, as she watched herself blow out all ten candles in one go on her birthday cake. She looked pretty, and so did the pink dress her mother had made for her. She remembered that dress and she remembered that day. She hadn't wanted it to end, and she hadn't wanted to take the dress off when it was time for bed.

The image faded, but Evie was eager to see what the next mirror held now. She was no longer afraid. She was beginning to like this room. It was bringing back such happy memories and she smiled as she turned to her left.

But the smile became a frown as another image appeared. The school netball pitch. Her at thirteen, and suddenly not so pretty. She remembered this day, when Linda Carstairs had called her fat and dumpy because she couldn't run as fast as the others and she was making them lose the match. It was only puppy fat, and temporary - a normal part of growing up her mother had told her - but to Evie it had felt like a life sentence, and it had hurt when everybody laughed at her. She'd cried all the way home from school, but the next morning she'd bought a fitness magazine and begged her mother for a new set of trainers. Six months later, and back to pretty and petite, she was the star of the netball team, and nobody ever laughed at her again. But she never forgot that horrible day when they did, and she was relieved when the image began to fade. She hoped the next mirror would show the pretty her again.

She stared into it as her image appeared, talking to Bartholomew Senior. She realised she was looking at a replay of this morning, when he'd told her about Beechcroft Manor and given her the keys. She looked away from it and towards the back of the room where the voice had come from.

There were only two mirrors left. What could they hold? She wasn't sure she wanted to find out.

Suddenly the voice spoke. 'Now you've seen your past Evie, it's time to look at your future. Ready?'

How could the voice ask her that? Of course, she wasn't ready. She didn't want to do this. She wanted to turn around and find the door had reappeared. And she wanted to run through it.

'But you can't run Evie.' How could the voice be so

inside her head, knowing her thoughts? 'Not until you know what you're running from. You wanted to see your past in the mirrors. Now you have the chance to see your future in them.'

'But there are only two mirrors left. I...' Her voice trailed off. She didn't want to go where that thought was taking her.

'Because there only needs to be two. How your future will start, and how it might end. Because the ending is up to you.'

Evie stood, motionless, barely able to breathe. She looked away from the mirrors. She didn't want to see any more images. She wanted to be back in the dark, airless hallway of Beechcroft Manor. Back in its sensory void and away from this room. Away from the light, the heavy scent of jasmine, the mirrors that held a destiny she didn't want to see, and a woman's voice she didn't want to hear.

But the woman was speaking again.

'Don't you want the chance to influence what the future holds Evie? A unique chance to change one thing? One thing that will decide your destiny. And the destiny of someone you will one day love more than you can possibly imagine now.'

As the voice paused Evie heard a key turn in a lock. She swung round to see the door had reappeared. It clicked open to reveal the darkness of the house that lay beyond it. This was her chance to escape. But now she wasn't sure she should.

'The room is giving you a choice Evie. Leave now and let destiny run its course. Or stay and decide how you want it to be.'

Evie turned away from the door and looked into the two blank mirrors. There was no decision to make. She had to stay and protect whoever was out there in her future. Whatever it took.

She spoke with an authority she'd never felt before in her life.

'Show me the first mirror.'

She gazed at both mirrors as her image appeared in one. She was wearing a wedding dress and turning to the man next to her as he took her hand. She saw his face and knew instantly who he was. Robert. Mr. Tinder. As she looked at him more closely, she knew she'd been right to like him at first sight on her phone screen. He was The One. Through the glass of the mirror she fell in love with him and felt his love for her. As she watched him slip the gold band on her finger the image faded, and another appeared in its place. She was in a hospital bed, holding a baby wrapped in a pink blanket. Robert's arm was draped around her and he was holding his daughter's hand with tears in his eyes.

Evie stood transfixed in front of the mirror and tried to blink back her own tears. Tears full of a joy that almost overwhelmed her as she watched. She wanted this joy for real. She wanted this future. She needed to be away from here, messaging Robert, making sure she didn't lose him. She had to make this future happen.

The image of them both with their new baby didn't fade like the others had, but her gaze was forced away from it as an image appeared in the final mirror. She gasped and her hand shot to her mouth as the image came into focus.

A young woman in a coffin. A young woman who looked a lot like her. She feared she knew who it was even before she made herself ask the question.

'Who is she? And how old is...was...she?'

'She's who you think she is, Evie. Your daughter. And she's twenty-six. A tragically early and unforeseen death.'

Evie screamed at the voice. 'God no. This can't happen. How could you make me see this?'

'Because you have the power to change it.'

'Just tell me how! Please! I'll do anything. I have to stop this! She can't die.'

'There is only one way you can stop this. You must smash the mirror. But there'll be a consequence Evie. Are you prepared for that?'

'I don't care about the consequence. Any price is worth paying to save her.'

'Then look down at your feet. Do what you have to do, then leave here. As quickly as you can.'

Evie tore her gaze from the haunting image, bent down and picked up the hammer that had appeared. She stared back at the other image, at her holding the baby daughter she was destined to give birth to and already knew she had to protect. Then she ran towards the final mirror, desperate to smash the image of that same daughter lying dead. She raised the hammer in both hands, then slammed it against the glass with a force she hadn't known she possessed.

As glass shards shot in all directions, she caught a brief glimpse of a figure moving beyond the shattered mirror. The woman didn't speak, but in the split second before she disappeared into the shadows, they made eye contact, and Evie knew who she was.

The room suddenly felt cold, the light started to fade, and the scent of jasmine disappeared. Evie dropped the hammer, turned, and ran towards the door. But she took one last look at the mirrors. Now they all held the same image. An older Robert, the daughter she'd seen in the coffin - now very much alive and smiling - and a baby wrapped in a pink blanket. Three generations, but with one person missing.

Her.

She reached the door as the light finally went out and the room was shrouded in darkness. She opened it and ran into the hallway of Beechcroft Manor. All the lights were on. She turned back to look at the third door, but it was gone.

She leaned against the wall and clutched her head against an attack of dizziness. Then she felt herself falling to the floor as she passed out.

Evie Whittaker plumped up the last two cushions on the sofa, flicked on the lamps, and switched on the flame-effect fire. She looked around the room and admired her efforts. It needed one last finishing touch. She sprayed a few mists of her favourite room fragrance into the air, breathed in the heady aroma of jasmine, and smiled. Now everything was perfect for the party later. She glanced at her watch. 6 o'clock. Robert would be home any minute and Juliet, Nick and the baby would here in an hour. Time to take her medication, then do one more job before she got changed. 'Slight heart murmur', the doctor had said at her check-up six months ago. Nothing too serious, provided she took her meds and regular breaks.

She headed to the kitchen, swallowed the two pills and turned her attention to the cake sitting on its silver stand on the worktop. She'd made a cake for Juliet's birthday every year, but she was particularly proud of this one. For once, she'd actually made a decent job of piping her daughter's name. For the past twenty-five years it had been an annual source of amusement to everybody that she never got the letters quite straight, but this year she'd given herself more time and she smiled with satisfaction at the result. She unwrapped the numeral candles she'd bought, and with the pink two and six in pride of place on top of the cake, she turned to go upstairs.

As she walked through the hallway she reflected, as she so often did, on the first time she'd seen it. All those years ago as a trainee at "Bartholomew & Bartholomew", long since closed, another victim of online estate agency. She remembered how she'd hated this dark, airless hallway when she first walked into it. But how, when the lights had inexplicably come on, they'd breathed life into it just before she fainted.

She'd put that down to tiredness and low blood sugar after a late night and no breakfast. Thank goodness her friend Annabel had called her to talk about New Year's Eve plans or she might have slept the entire afternoon away on the tiled floor of Beechcroft Manor. Instead she'd made it back to the office with time for a detour to buy that red dress she'd been thinking about since the weekend.

It was still hanging in her wardrobe, even after all these years, a memento of the night she met Robert. She couldn't bear to part with it, although she smiled at the thought of trying to fit into it now. But it had worked its magic on him. As the clock had struck midnight to herald in a new year, he'd taken her in his arms, told her this was his last ever first date, and that she was quite the most beautiful thing he'd ever seen. She'd looked into his face and known this was the man she would marry. And suddenly Colville no longer felt dull.

And here she was, thirty years later, still living in Beechcroft Manor. Something she could never have imagined, until Robert had brought her here, three months after they met - on the same day he asked her to marry him - and presented her with a diamond ring and a key.

Now, as she walked upstairs to their room, anticipating

him being home any moment, she felt the familiar warm glow that she always got when she thought of him, even after so many years of marriage. She walked into the room and on impulse opened her wardrobe to touch the red dress. She had so much to thank this dress for.

She sat on the bed, suddenly feeling tired. It had been a long day, but a good one. Excited at the thought of the evening ahead, her head dropped towards the pillow. A ten-minute nap would do her good before the party. Robert would wake her up in plenty of time.

~

She woke up feeling cold, still on the bed. Robert was lying next to her holding her hand, but she sensed other people in the room too. She tried to talk, but nobody seemed to hear her. She got up from the bed and walked to the door. She felt oddly weightless as if her feet were barely making contact with the floor.

She turned back and saw herself still lying on the bed. Paramedics were leaning over, alternately thumping and massaging her chest and holding an oxygen mask to her face. Robert was still next to her, holding her hand and saying her name. Juliet stood at the foot of the bed, watching and crying as she was being held by her husband.

Evie watched the scene, feeling strangely calm. She knew any moment the paramedics would give up. She already knew they were wasting their time. She didn't want to be there when they told Robert and Juliet they could do no more, it was time to stop, so she slipped out of the room. At the top of the stairs she looked down at the hallway. It was in darkness, just like the first time she saw it all those years ago.

But half way down she saw the light. It was guiding her towards a door. And she remembered. And, finally, she understood.

She pushed the door open, knowing what she would find. She closed it behind her, walked into the room and there were the mirrors. The mirrors she'd looked into so many years ago. But they all were blank, and none was broken.

She walked through them and saw the empty chair beyond them. As she moved towards it, she thought of Juliet upstairs. The most precious thing she'd ever held in her life. Her daughter was sad now, of course, but the sadness would gradually fade, as the joy in her future took over. The wonderful future she would have with her new husband and baby. A life full of opportunity, that might never have happened.

Evie smiled even though she wouldn't be part of that future. Not for a while at least. She sat down in the glow of the lamp. For now, all she could do was wait.

Until the third door opened again.

A NOTE FROM CHARLOTTE

Thank you for reading *LATE NIGHT SHOTS.*

I HOPE you enjoyed my three stories, and the story from Laura Cation, who I have been delighted to introduce.

I WILL BE WORKING on *LATE NIGHT SHOTS* 2 soon and plan to feature a new writer in that collection too. If you're an aspiring (as yet unpublished) writer yourself and would like to see your story included, sign up to my Readers' Community using the link on my website (details below) - for future details of my next Writing Challenge.

ALONGSIDE WRITING SHORT STORIES, I am a novelist, and my debut novel *THE CERBERUS AFFAIR* was published in May 2020. It is a conspiracy thriller, set in the world of cutting-edge genetics research. A mysterious organisation threatens to derail a ground-breaking discovery that could change human life forever. One woman is determined to protect it - whatever the risk. It is available on all Amazon stores in paperback or eBook.

BUILDING a relationship with my readers is important to me, so to contact me - or for more information about me and my writing - please visit my website at:-

www.charlottevalentinewriter.com

Please hit the link on the website to join my reader community and receive exclusive free reading content and early information about forthcoming releases.

FINALLY, I hope you will take a few moments to share your thoughts on *LATE NIGHT SHOTS* with others by leaving a review on Amazon.

THANK you again for reading my first collection of short stories.

ABOUT THE AUTHOR

Charlotte Valentine was born and grew up in the north of England then studied law in London. She worked in investment banking before deciding to pursue her love of literature and study for her MA with the Open University. This inspired her to write.

While completing a Creative Writing course, she began writing short stories and planning her first novel. That novel became *The Cerberus Affair* which was published in May 2020 and two of those short stories were the foundation for *Late Night Shots*, her second publication in August 2020.

Now a full-time writer, she splits her time between London and southern Spain where she shares her home with her teenage son, 8 rescued cats and a dog.

For more information:

www.charlottevalentinewriter.com

ACKNOWLEDGMENTS

This book could not have been written and published without the support and help of others, and this is my opportunity to thank them.

I am indebted as always to Anna – my technical guru, marketing adviser and, above all, friend. All the credit for formatting *LATE NIGHT SHOTS* for publication, and for designing and producing the cover goes to her – with my gratitude.

My thanks to those people who read the stories before I decided to publish them. Your positive comments and encouragement gave me the confidence to include them in this collection. You know who you are.

To my son, Alex, for living with the strange hours I kept in the final production stages of this book, and for his culinary expertise which kept me well fed!

And, finally, to the four-legged people who share our

home and my writing space; our dog and cats. They continually show me unconditional love and the value of balancing confidence with humility.

Charlotte V.

Printed in Great Britain
by Amazon

48521798R00052